C. E Johnstone

Ballads of Boy and Beak

C. E Johnstone

Ballads of Boy and Beak

ISBN/EAN: 9783742899705

Manufactured in Europe, USA, Canada, Australia, Japa

Cover: Foto ©Andreas Hilbeck / pixelio.de

Manufactured and distributed by brebook publishing software
(www.brebook.com)

C. E Johnstone

Ballads of Boy and Beak

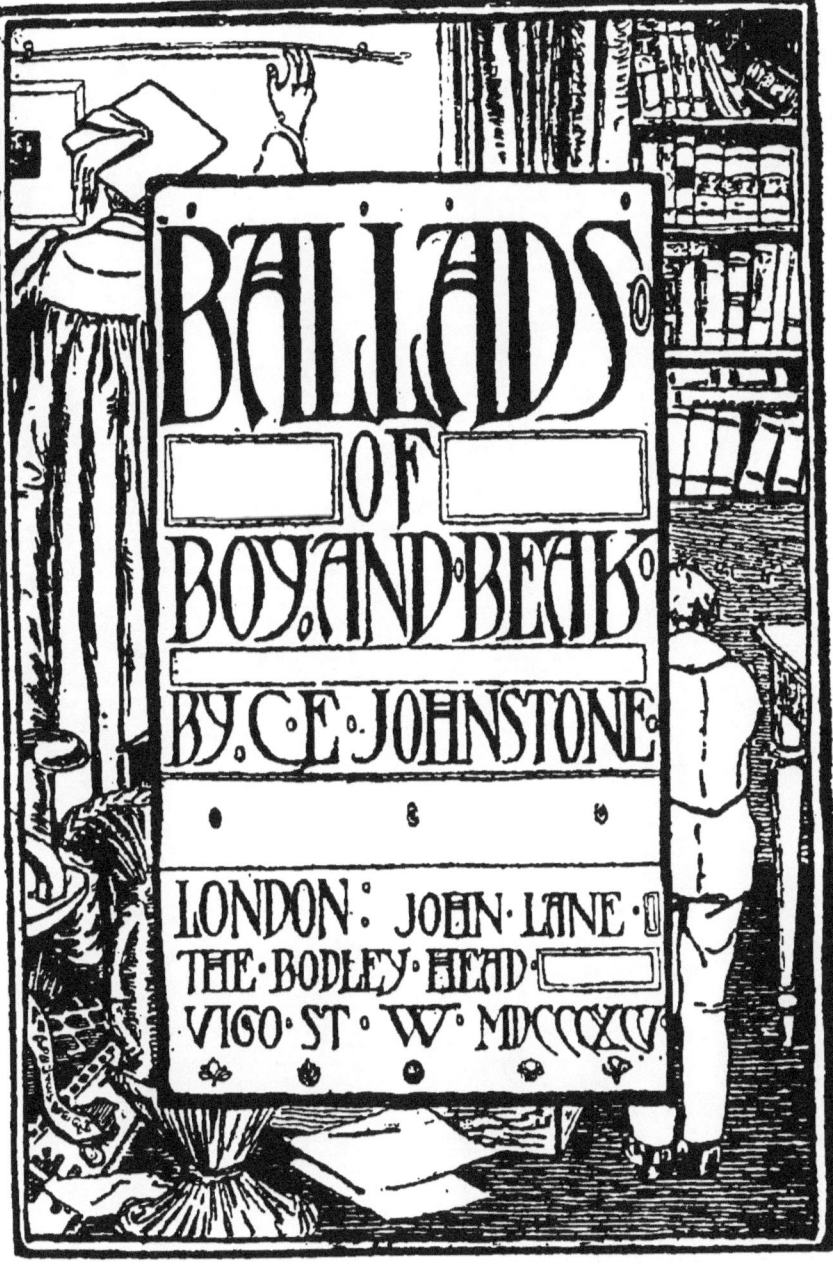

BALLADS

OF

BOY·AND·BEAK

BY·C·E·JOHNSTONE

LONDON: JOHN·LANE
THE·BODLEY·HEAD
VIGO·ST·W·MDCCCXCV

J. Miller and Son, Printers, Edinburgh

UNLINKED by any ties of kin
  I chanced into your caravan,
You entertained and took me in—
  No angel, but a prickly man.

You made me welcome to your best,
  And gave me, stranger and unknown,
As brother rather than as guest,
  A home more homelike than my own.

If to my sight have been unfurled
  Some glimpses of the point of view,
From which the boy surveys the world,
  I learnt it every whit from you.

From you and from your Mother—she
  Whose gentle influence controlled
With guiding hand we did not see,
  And touch that turned our dross to gold.

For idle tongues, that scattered free
  Their froth of gossip fleck'd with gall,
Would hush their chatter to agree—
  ' She sits apart above us all.'

You never show'd by word or sign,
  That boyish faults had power to fray
Your patience at its edge, when mine
  Wore threadbare twenty times a day.

I

Your only fault to one who scann'd
  A critic eager to complain,
That when you smote you stay'd your hand,
  And halv'd the necessary pain.

Upon your slowly circling wheel
  You strive to work your vessels pure
Of flaw and blemish, and anneal
  Their temper, steadfast to endure.

Kind potter, yours the patient skill,
  And tireless fingers deft to train,
And mould the mind and wakening will
  Their part hereafter to sustain.

Alas ! as up life's hill they. trudge,
  If one should stumble in the dust,
He will not find another judge
  As patient, and as kindly just !

UPON the world's capacious lap
    I cast my book—a tiny scrap—
        To push and jostle for a place
        In the mad scurry of life's race ;
If it can find some humble gap.

'Poor fool ! Their fingers men will snap
At this in scorn, nor care a rap ;
        Your book will die and leave no trace
           Upon the world

This is your honest *verbum sap ?*
What then ?   It were no great mishap.
        I never dream'd I should outpace
        The rest in beauty, wit or grace ;
Nor burst—a deafening thunder-clap
           Upon the world !

TWO BOYS

A YOUTH of high degree,
  His wavy locks well *smalmed* with redolent
    cosmetic,
Who goes, like Agag, somewhat mincingly—
  'Bad form to seem too energetic!'

An oily placid smirk
  Plays softly round the cherub's angel features,
To show the scorn that in his heart must lurk
  For all his paltry fellow-creatures.

.   .   .   .

A chubby, grubby, boy,
  Whose face and collar frequent drops of ink be-
    spatter.
Mere dirt cannot his happiness destroy,
  Whose motto is 'It doesn't matter.'

His rebel hair is rough.
  With tie ill-tied, and boots both innocent of laces,
His fingers 'sicklied o'er' with sugar stuff.
  His only art is making faces.

.   .   .   .

  The one 'a little dear,'
His mother says, nor marks his most offensive
    swagger,
  The other, no such paragon I fear,
But just 'a jolly little beggar.'

4

FATUOUS, fussy, severe,
   Thinning the trouser by friction ;
Prone to the box on the ear—
  Such is the master in fiction.
  Primly precise in his diction,
When he proses (more vulgarly ' gasses.')
  Impressed with the rooted conviction
That boys are unspeakable asses.

This is all very well as a hit
  Of the kind that is known as rhetorical ;
Yet we're bound as a fact to admit,
  That the portrait is scarcely historical.
  Squeers is no longer the oracle,
Nor that portly old fraud Dr Grimstone.
  They have passed into realms allegorical,
Along with the treacle and brimstone.

Resolute, manly, and kind,
  Striking awe to the heart of the lurker ;
A fell nemesis, ever behind
  The slow, shuffling steps of the shirker.
  No invertebrate, plausible smirker ;
But honest, alert, energetic ;
  A patient, untiring worker—
Strong, yet withal sympathetic.

5

In the dust of a kindlier age
   Lies the tomahawk buried for ever ;
And no more shall hostility rage
   'Twixt the taught and the tutor.   For never
   Shall mortal be found to endeavour
To promote such a signal disaster,
   As the friendly relations to sever,
Which now bind the boy to the master.

WHEN bowed by the breath of the breezes,
    Thou bendest thy head to the sky,
Thy traceried elegance pleases
    Both the crude and the critical eye.
Thou art peerless, unmatched, tho' creation
    Be ransacked with the strictest research !
Then to thee let us pour a libation,
    O beautiful birch !

Oh curly and crisp and caressing
    Is the lingering lick of the cane ;
As it clings, an equivocal blessing,
    To the sufferer writhing in pain.
Has one failed in his duties scholastic ?
    Is he rude, insubordinate, slack ?
Then sinuous, lithe, and elastic
    It falls on his back.

The ash-plant, abrupt and aggressive,
    Is clumsy, and raises a lump ;
And the pain it produces excessive,
    As is also the case with a stump.
Epidermis is apt to be made dough
    By the fives-bat's too forcible flout;
Which is worse than the brute bastinado,
    Or barbarous knout.

AD
BE(A)TULAM

7

Objections to that and to this stick
    Are freely and frequently raised ;
But the birch is humane and artistic;
    And can never too highly be praised.
For making the cuticle tender,
    What better could anyone wish,
Than the tremulous twigs of the slender
    And delicate swish ?

So the Sybarite scion of Eton
    Treats thee, fitly, with reverent awe
Whene'er by thy boughs he is beaten,
    And his back rendered rosily raw,
His sense of thy charms not yet fled, dead,
    He gracefully yields thee thy due ;
And ties thee up over his bed-head,
    In ribbons of blue.

MY private school, elect, serene,
    To you I went, when young and green ;
  And learned, from your injunctions strict,
  That 'it is rude to contradict,'
And 'boys should not be heard when seen.'

The soap-like cheese, the chill sardine,
And thin-spread oleo-margarine,
  Still aid my memory to depict
      My private school.

They'd run with pots of *vaseline*,
And plasters of *pommade divine*,
  If one his little finger pricked,
  Of harshness you could ne'er convict
That grand-maternal teach-machine—
    My private school !

9

BALLADE OF THE MILD USHER

IF your boys only do as they're told,
  It is all very well to be kind,
On the plan of the people who hold
    That small boys as a race are maligned ;
    But as soon as they see you're inclined
To let minor delinquencies pass,
    As a ruler your death-warrant's signed—
They will think you a thundering ass.

When you mildly admonish and scold,
  It is clearly their duty to mind,
But they don't—and you feel you are sold,
    And have wasted your words on the wind.
    For an average boy you will find
Has a scorn, that is harder than brass,
    For a threat which has nothing behind,
And will think you a thundering ass.

And they promptly grow cheeky and bold
  When they 'twig' that you're calmly resigned
To the fact that they're badly controlled ;
    And your discipline's then undermined.
    If your wrath to mere 'jaw' is confined,
They will reckon you greener than grass,
    Unless pain with reproof is combined,
They will think you a thundering ass.

10

Envoy

Mild usher, your method refined
   Doesn't really go down with your class,
Who will merely suppose you are blind,
   And will think you a thundering ass.

I T needs no great ambition to aspire
    To teach the British boy his A, B, C,
It does not take a very brilliant flyer
    To drum at *mensa*, or the *rule of three*,
    You merely want a 'Varsity degree,
(It is not hard to shuffle through the schools !)
    To make you all a pedagogue should be ;
For any fool can teach a pack of fools.

A scathing tongue is what you most require—
    The not uncommon gift of repartee ;
The knack of hinting that a boy's a liar,
    While seeming to applaud his probity.
    Or, if a boy should dare to disagree
With what you say, a sneer is cheap, and cools
    His ardour, and cuts short his rising glee ;
For any fool can teach a pack of fools.

The man who's judged it prudent to retire
    From making tombstones, or retailing tea ;
Or failed in his endeavour to acquire
    A practice as a lawyer or M.D.
    The man who's chucked away his last half ' d '
In backing horses, or in ' option pools—'
    Who better fitted for the post than he ?
For any fool can teach a pack of fools.

12

Envoy

You do not think so ?   Ask A. G. & T.,
  In Sackville Street, enthroned upon their stools ;
I think you'll find them ready to agree
  That any fool can teach a pack of fools.

AN USHER'S
DUTIES.
A BALLADE
FROM
ANOTHER
POINT OF
VIEW

WHATEVER tasks they should fulfil,
    Alike the toilsome and the light—
To set about them with a will,
    And work at them with all their might.
    Thinking no shame to take delight
In practising what others preach ;
    To render sadder lives more bright—
These are the things you have to teach.

To choose the good, and shun the ill,
    Unfaltering and firm, in spite
Of busy mockers, who would chill
    The ardour of a faithful knight.
    To be both manly and polite,
And chivalrous in act and speech,
    To aid the weaker in the fight ;
These are the things you have to teach.

Pure tastes and manly to instil,
    High aspirations to excite ;
That, climbing up life's rocky hill,
    They may attain its snow-clad height
    With faces set to use aright
The talents God bestows on each,
    Until they pass into the night ;
These are the things you have to teach

14

Envoy

To strive with souls unsullied, white,
  Perfection's lofty goal to reach—
This is the aim to keep in sight ;
  These are the things you have to teach.

BALLADE OF BURDENS

THE burden of dull teaching. Small delight
    Cometh to one that toileth all the day,
Instructing brainless boys to read and write,
    And striving information to convey.
    For prematurely shall thy hair turn grey,
In fathoming their depths of dulness dire ;
    They know not now what they knew yesterday—
This is the end of every boy's desire.

The burden of much nagging ; when, in spite
    Of all thine exhortations to obey,
They disregard thy strict injunctions quite,
    And, when thou shoutest, look the other way.
    Thou to thyself strange oaths dost softly say,
Consigning them to nether realms of fire ;
    Yet hast no power to scourge them, nor to flay.
This is the end of every boy's desire.

The burden of much running ; when in sight
    Of all the boys at football thou dost play ;
And thy lean limbs, no longer nimbly light,
    Progress but slowly o'er the clinging clay.
    Then shall the heart of every boy wax gay,
While thou dost most unpleasantly perspire,
    And, on thy shins, their wrongs they shall repay,
This is the end of every boy's desire.

Envoy

Usher, be calm, thou wilt not find it pay,
  When baited, to give vent unto thine ire.
Thou shalt be sacked, and swiftly sent away,
  This is the end of every boy's desire.

HE t*h*ain dem in de way to go,
  Good mo*r*al p*r*ecepts he supply—
He teachee all dey b'long to know,
  How to subt*r*act and multiply.
  But dough his p*r*inciple's so high,
A*ll*anged upon a first-chop plan,
  His best inst*r*uction dey defy,
An'·g*r*ieve dat poor teach-pidgin-man.

He not hab muchee cash, galow !
  His purse *r*un often ve*ll*y d*r*y.
He not wear ve*ll*y top-side clo',
  For not affordee dem to buy.
  An' so dey winkee wid deir eye,
An' cockee Snook, wid out-sp*r*ead han',
  When his ole boots come bulgin' by ;
An' g*r*ieve dat poor teach-pidgin-man.

Dey th*r*owre pellets to an' f*r*o,
  An' chow-chow bulls eyes on de sly.
Or t*r*ead upon de teach-man's toe—
  Chop-chop ! He jump ! An' sc*r*eam out 'Hi !'
  An' den dey laugh until dey c*r*y,
An' fill his ink-pot up wid san'.
  To make him in a tant*r*um fly,
An' g*r*ieve dat poor teach-pidgin-man.

18

Envoy

Bad chilo ! when you know he t*l*y
  To help you eve*l*y way he can !
What for you make him g*h*unt an' sigh,
  An' g*h*ieve dat poor teach-pidgin-man ?

HE is not very good,
  Nor beautiful, nor wise;
Thinks more about his food
  Than of his boots and ties
  Affects not to despise
A periwinkle tea;
  And yet he's sure to rise,
He reads the B. O. P.

The sad subjunctive mood
  He hates, without disguise;
And fain would see tabooed
  All 'X's,' 'Z's,' and 'Y's.'
  Will he secure the prize?
He shakes his head.   'Not he!'
  And truthfully replies,
'*He* reads the B. O. P.'

He talks not of the flood,
  Nor of Queen Anne's demise;
Regards not Norman blood,
  Nor raves of hazel eyes
  At cocoa-nuts he shies,
Propels the nimble pea,
  And when their glamour dies
He reads the B. O. P.

20

Envoy

Is he a boy who tries
　To emulate the bee?
Who knows?　At least he buys
　And reads the B. O. P.

Y OU little *fool!*' I heard the tyrant say,
      (My fag-master to wit!) one luckless day,
    When I had blacked his toast, and made his tea
    With luke-warm water, burned his fricasee
To shrivelled cinders of a ghastly gray.

In wrath he spoke to me in deep dismay,
(I knew the tone too well to disobey).
'Just find my stick, and bring it here to me
            You little fool!'

With practised hand he then began to lay
That ash-plant on my back, nor did he stay
    His blows, till they had numbered three times
        three.
    Then, when a parting kick had set me free,
I muttered softly, as I sped away,
            'You *little* fool!'

NO! I don't think you'd call him acute!
    He is grossly and shamelessly slack,
The great thick-headed indolent brute.

If you ask him a question, he's mute,
    For of thinking he hasn't the knack.
No! I don't think you'd call him acute.

You may toil, but you'll gather no fruit.
    He is proof against culture's attack ;
The great thick-headed indolent brute.

Why he can't tell Cavour from Canute,
    Nor a tenpenny nail from a tack !
No! I don't think you'd call him acute.

And you long, with the toe of your boot,
    To admonish his obstinate back,
The great thick-headed indolent brute.

He is calm, tho' you thunder and hoot,
    And unmoved, tho' you batter and whack !
No! I don't think you'd call him acute,
The great thick-headed indolent brute !

23

THERE goes that brute of a bell!
    Jove, what a shindy it makes!
I call it a regular sell
    To hear such a row when one wakes.

Jove, what a shindy it makes—
    Everyone starting to dress!
To hear such a row when one wakes,
    Is more beastly than words can express.

Everyone starting to dress?
    Getting-up is no end of a bore,
It's more beastly than words can express,
    I shall lie here a few minutes more.

Getting-up is no end of a bore,
    It's a thing I most heartily hate.
I shall lie here a few minutes more,
    But, my goodness! I mustn't be late.

It's a thing I most heartily hate.
    To turn out of a jolly warm bed ;
But, my goodness! I mustn't be late,
    I don't want to get six from the Head.

To turn out of a jolly warm bed—
    Well, it's healthy, I've always been told.
I don't want to get six from the Head,
    So here goes—brrr! It's horribly cold!

24

Well it's healthy, I've always been told,
  When your tub is all covered with ice,
So here goes—brrr ! It's horribly cold !
  I call it too dear at the price.

When your tub is all covered with ice
  Every nerve in your body it numbs.
I call it too dear at the price,
  When your fingers all freeze into thumbs.

Every nerve in your body it numbs !
  How on earth can you do up your boots
When your fingers all freeze into thumbs ?
  Out comes the lace by the roots.

How on earth can you do up your boots
  In the twentieth part of a minute ?
Out comes the lace by the roots !
  Oh, where is my stud ! I must pin it.

In the twentieth part of a minute
  I shall get in a jolly good row !
Oh, where *is* my stud ? I must pin it.
  Blow ! it's all up with me now !

I shall get in a jolly good row !
  I call it a regular sell !
Blow ! It's all up with me now !
  There goes that brute of a bell !

OH, soft is the fluff
  Of the eider-down bird ;
Soft is putty ; nor tough
  The white Syllabub-curd.
Soft the *scwug* of a roll,
  But far softer the stuff
Which composes the soul
  Of the Sweet Little Muff.

' Hi there, come out and play ! ' from the football-
    field calling
  Sounds the voice of the monitor, angry and gruff.
' To the front, where the forwards are shoving and
    mauling !
  Why don't you join them, my Sweet Little
    Muff ? '

' My mamma says,' lisps the darling in answer,
  ' Football is dangerous, brutal and rough
I much prefer a refined little dance, sir.
  That's why I shirk,' says the Sweet Little Muff.

' And besides, I might dirty my velveteen knickers,
  Or injure my little brown billy-cock hat,
If I ventured too near to those violent kickers ;
  So I'd rather look on,' says the Slack Little Brat.

26

'Tis a fine excuse truly ! Was ever a worse made ?
  Go and get him his little pink coral to suck !
Bring him his push-waggon, send for his nurse-
    maid,
  Wheel him home gently, the Sweet Little Duck !

Give him the *crocodile* dear to the girls' school,
  Dress'd in his best ; and to save him from tan,
A sunshade to keep his complexion and curls cool ;
  Then he'll be happy, the Sweet Little Man !

Vain are the vaunted allurements of cricket,
  For the slowest long hop to bowl *him* is enough !
What does he care for the fall of his wicket ?
  'Three silly sticks ! ' says the Smart Little Muff.

Unknown to him the delight of a *sixer*,
  Or the smartly held catch, with its tingling joy.
No, the Noah's Ark and a nice box of bricks, sir,
  Are more in the line of *this* Sweet Little Boy.

Get his small sister to teach him cat's-cradle,
  Or to pat the light shuttlecock over a net ;
Or puss-in-the-corner—but that I'm afraid 'll
  Perhaps prove too rough for the Sweet Little Pet

27

In the winter, when all other schoolboys are skating,
   Or merrily sliding, as hard as they can,
And even mamma says, 'Dear, why are you
      waiting?'
   ' 'Cause I might tumble down,' says the Sweet
   Little Man.

In the summer the darling has got to be fann'd!
   Box
   Him up in the winter from wind and from wet;
Then, in cotton-wool wrapped, pack him up in a
   band-box,
   And label him 'breakable'—Sweet Little Pet.

Let others toil hard to win honour and glory
   For their school and themselves; but it's perfectly
      clear
To his dear little mind that such things are a bore.
   He
   ' Prefers to look on,' says the Sweet Little Dear.

Bring him a little tin-trumpet and rattle,
   Or a wax-featured doll, stuff'd with sawdust or
      bran.
Then, while his brothers are fighting life's battle,
   Rock him to sleep, the Dear, Sweet, Little Man.

I T was not called a school. Oh no !
      That word was always reckoned low
At 'Culture House Academy,
Dove Road, St. Muggleton-on-Sea.'

They did not speak of 'masters ' there—
Name fraught with tyranny and fear ;
But called them, as more musical,
'Instructors' and 'the Principal.'

The Reverend Doctor Coddleton
Believed himself by nature one
Especially designed to rule
A happy high-class private school.

His voice was unctuous and bland,
He had a soft caressing hand,
'Which never,' so he'd boast with joy
'Had struck a poor defenceless boy.'

'Boy,' did I say ? most vulgar word
Suggestive of the common herd.
It was of course a slip of pen,
For these were all 'young gentlemen.'

No low-bred slang their speech debased,
But phrases their remarks prefaced
Like ' have the goodness,' 'should you mind ? '
Or ' would you be so very kind ? '

BOARDING-
SCHOOL
BALLADS—
I. THE
REFINED
ACADEMY

29

They used no nicknames, which reveal
A type of mind most ungenteel;
But spoke with gentle emphasis
Of ' master' that, and ' mister' this.

Their well-oiled locks were never rough,
None ever showed a dirty cuff ;
But all had patent-leather boots,
And always wore their Sunday suits.

Rough games like football they declined,
As quite unfit for youths refined,
But played at cricket (if you call
It cricket !) with a woolly ball.

But mostly they preferred to go
For promenades correct and slow,
Linked arm in arm on the Parade,
In spotless ties and gloves arrayed.

Where now and then the passers-by
(Low creatures !) winked the other eye,
And asked each other with a smile
The masculine of ' crocodile.'

Then in the evenings they would sit
In graceful attitudes, and knit ;
Or else reclined in easy chairs,
And worked at little canvas squares.

·   ·   ·   ·

Into this happy little world,
One melancholy day was hurled
By fortune, who we know is blind,
A youth of quite a different kind.

No lily-handed scion he
Of cultured aristocracy ;
But boorish, blatant, loud and rude,
Of manners quite unformed and crude.

His plain plebeian name was Dick—
A fact which galled them to the quick—
Those St. Clares, Esmés, Egertons,
Veres, Montagues, and Algernons.

He'd dig them in the ribs, and tweak
Their ears, to make the darlings shriek ;
Or showed, while they for mercy prayed,
How barley-sugar should be made.

He neither cared for youth nor age,
But all alike he would enrage
By calling them insulting names
(A trick which oft low birth proclaims).

The boys were 'mammy's brats' or 'smugs,'
They had, he said, such 'pretty mugs ;'
And called (whereat their marrow froze !)
The principal 'Old Coddletoes,'

But worse than all he clean defied
All rules ; and when the Doctor tried
To reason with him, bade him go
To Bath ; and even dared—but no.

Let me not soil this blameless pen,
By writing where he ventured then
To place, with fingers spread, his thumb.
I draw the veil—shocked page be dumb.

His tears, at such defiance plain,
The principal could scarce restrain ;
But said, with eyes dimmed by their mist
' Can wickedness like this exist ? '

' Unhappy infant, doomed to shame
Your parents, and their honoured name,
Go.   From your baleful presence free
Outraged St. Muggleton-on-sea.'

' Not much, old cock,' replied the youth,
' I'll stay and cut my wisdom tooth ;
Gee swee, gee rest, beyond a doubt,
Unless you're going to "chuck me out "' '

With dignity the Doctor rose,
And, standing in a stately pose,
(While through the room a flutter ran),
He rang the bell for Mary Ann

32

When she arrived, he thus began—
' Kindly oblige me, Mary Ann,
By going out at once to find
A constable—a smart one, mind.'

She very shortly reappeared,
And this time in her wake she steered,
In regulation suit of blue,
Stout constable M. 32.

' Policeman,' thus the doctor spake,
' This juvenile offender take ;
Convey him back to this address,
And rid us of his wickedness.'

Then turning to the boy went on :
' Richard, reflect when you are gone
Upon the blessings you this day
So recklessly have thrown away.

' You might at length have learned to feel
How sweet it is to be genteel ;
And so in time have grown to be
A type of true nobility.

' But now your chance you have resigned
Of " good " companionship refined.
Depart at once without delay ;
Policeman, take the youth away.'

The constable, with visage calm.
Surveyed the sovereign in his palm ;
Yet failed his proper course to trace
In such an unfamiliar case.

But while he stood, in doubt involved,
The boy himself the problem solved;
By jumping up with the remark,
' Come on then, Bobby, here's a lark ! '

When they, admitting their defeat,
Had fared into the silent street,
The Doctor turned, and thus addressed
The boys, who still appeared distressed.

' Dear youths, this painful incident
A pang through all our hearts has sent ;
And, as our minds have been thus taxed
The work to-day shall be relaxed.

I will give orders to the maid
To bring you in some lemonade;
And a mixed-biscuit too may serve
To readjust the shattered nerve.'

.   .   .   .   .   .

Once more in its accustomed groove
The life at ' Culture House ' can move
And undisturbed tranquillity
Reigns at St. Muggleton-on-Sea.

THE hero of this little tale
　　Was never known to jump or run ;
His countenance was round and pale,
　　His name was Thomas Stowgington.

His hair was of a flaming red,
　　(Called auburn by his dear mamma),
He loved his victuals and his bed,
　　And had no wish to see the Shah.

No, his ambition did not soar,
　　Its formula was short and sweet.
' True happiness is having more
　　Than one can reasonably eat.'

No visions thronged before his eyes
　　Of future greatness, world-wide fame.
His dreams were all of pigeon-pies,
　　To fill his waistcoat was his aim.

But, while for quantity he yearned,
　　Mere common food he could not bear.
His sybaritish spirit spurned
　　The plainness of scholastic fare.

The bread and butter he would blame,
　　And call it *alum margarine*,
(Of course he ate it all the same,
　　Else had his figure grown more lean).

35

Tom's squidgy nose towards the sky
  (His mother deemed the feature Greek!)
Would curl at 'resurrection pie,'
  And compounds known as 'bubble and squeak.'

He said the beef was 'tram-car horse,'
  The mutton, 'donkey,' 'bootsole,' 'trash,'
The *haricot* in language coarse
  He termed 'tinned missionary hash.'

Great then was Thomas's delight,
  To learn that there had come for him
A hamper, on the previous night,
  Packed full with dainties to the brim.

Therein reclined a portly ham,
  A round-faced tongue, and many a score
Of oranges and pots of jam,
  A truly appetising store.

Now when the news had got about
  That such a 'heap of grub' had come,
They crowded round him, crying out
  'I say, old Stowgy, I'm your chum.'

Then poured in offers thick and fast,
  Of knives and other instruments,
To portion out a rich repast,
  From these magnificent contents.

36

Unmoved their clamour Thomas heard,
  (A truly solid youth was he !)
' He would not trespass,' he averred,
  ' Upon their generosity.'

' The grub,' he ventured to suppose
  ' Was his.   He did not care a pin ;
And he should use it as he chose,
  And failed to see where they came in.'

The hamper then he raised on high,
  And, staggering beneath its weight,
With triumph gleaming in his eye
  He calmly shuffled off, elate.

His purpose was his prize to bear
  Into some corner screened from view,
Where scanty crumbs might, here and there
  Be doled to a selected few.

For since he never felt inclined
  Towards being lavish or profuse,
The greater portion in his mi d
  He destined for his private use.

But tho' he knew it not, unkind
  Relentless fate was on his track ;
Black care was creeping close behind
  His sorely over-burdened back.

Scenting some mischief from afar
  The matron first the scene surveyed,
Then sternly swooped, in time to mar
  The little plans T. S. had laid.

Just when our friend had ceased to fear
  That now his scheme could go amiss,
Her strident voice broke on his ear—
  'Why, Master Stowgington! What's this?

'A lot of food! Well, I declare!
  No hampers to be sent to school.
You cannot fail to be aware
  That this has always been the rule.'

But' argued Thomas, 'hitherto
  The rule has not been put in force.'
'Now hold your tongue, you rude boy, do!
  To argue only makes it worse!'

Then like some ruthless bird of prey
  She calmly carried off the prize;
While Thomas stood in blank dismay,
  And watched it go with longing eyes.

She bore it to her room with joy,
  (Tho' breathless, being somewhat stout;)
'I've long disliked that horrid boy,'
  She panted, 'now I've paid him out.'

Within her room that night was laid
    An elegant and dainty spread,
Whereat her friends the lady's maid
    And butler sumptuously fed.

But Thomas, of his grub bereft
    In solitary silence mourned,
(Like Dido), till the plumpness left
    His cheeks, which hollows now adorned.

Yet as he slender grew, and thin
    A wondrous change in him was wrought.
The slacker seemed to change his skin,
    His limbs grew strong, and muscles taut.

His mind, which once despised all claims,
    Save those which to his greed appealed,
Now lightly turned to thoughts of games,
    And deeds of prowess in the field.

Such names as ' dumpling,' ' butter-tub,'
    They cannot call him now with truth.
No—Stowgington they rightly dub,
    A handsome and agreeable youth.

Of athletes he is now the pride,
    He runs the hundred like a hare,
To see him o'er the hurdles stride
    Would cause a kangaroo to stare !

39

So, first alike in work and sport,
    By lofty aspirations fired,
His conduct, (*vide* school report),
    ' Leaves nothing now to be desired.'

Moral

Good boys will doubtless notice how
    Disaster in advantage ends ;
Since Thomas Stowgington is now
    A credit to himself and friends.

And clever ones will comprehend
    That it is never right (nor wise)
The matron's feelings to offend,
    Nor cause her Jove-like wrath to rise.

I F you wish for his name.
　And approximate weight,
It was Slogger.　The same,
　I regret to relate,
Was a hulking inveterate bully,
　Who scaled about thirteen stone eight.

Wearing large patterned bags,
　Smoking secret cheroots,
The suppression of fags—
　Were his chosen pursuits,
Hence he carried an overgrown ash-plant
　And wore large, anatomical boots.

But the worm has been known
　On occasion to turn ;
Even fags, tho' not prone
　To vendetta, will yearn
To take points off a bully who labours
　Too keenly their hatred to earn.

So they met and resolved
　To throw off, by intrigue,
Slogger's yoke, which involved
　So much pain and fatigue ;
And they formed themselves into a union
　Called, *The Fags' indivisible League*.

Nevermore to obey
　(Resolution the first)
His injunctions.　Were they
　To be tamely coerced
By this brute? No! they hurled their defiance
　In his teeth, and prepared for the worst.

They proceeded to toss,
　With a view to decide
Who, as chairman or boss,
　O'er the league should preside ;
And the lot fell on Jenkinson minor,
　Who was straightway uplifted with pride.

On the wriggling point
　Of a corkscrew they swore,
By their hardships conjoint,
　That henceforth nevermore
Would they eat either bulls-eyes or toffee,
　Till their vengeance had smitten him sore.

So it happened next day,
　When he called for a fag,
That none came to obey,
　Save the voice of a wag,
Who advised him to try shouting louder,
　Or to signal by waving a flag.

Then in wrath he uprose,
  And fared forth in pursuit.
On the ears of his foes
  Fell his furious hoot,
Like the trumpet-note calling to battle
  The nervous, but eager, recruit.

When he first came in sight,
  They all deemed it discreet
To betake them to flight,
  Being speedy of feet ;
But a smile played round Jenkinson's features,
  As he gracefully led the retreat.

Slogger, dumpy and stout,
  Large of waist, double-chinned,
Soon stopped running, to shout,
  (Whereat all of them grinned)
Awful threats of most horrible tortures
  Being longer of tongue than of wind.

Then the fugitive group
  Turned and faced him at bay ;
With one ear-splitting ' whoop ! '
  They rushed straight for their prey,
And Slogger saw stars for a moment,
  Then prostrate and motionless lay.

43

That his perfect repose
  Might be fully assured,
With stout whip-cord his toes
  And his hands they secured,
While Jenkinson playfully gagged him,
  With a tennis-ball, somewhat matured.

Next they held a *durbar*
  Sitting round on his shins ;
And to feather and tar
  Him resolved for his sins ;
So they carefully tarred him with treacle,
  And feathered him over with whins.

And they pinned to his breast
  An inscription, or brand,
That was fitly expressed
  With magniloquence grand ;
And their president, Jenkinson, signed it
  In an elegant copy-book hand.

' Pause stranger, and wait
  Till you realise well
The deplorable fate,
  Which here swiftly befell
One who rashly incurred the displeasure
  Of the *F's indivisible L.'*

Then they hurried away,
    Leaving Slogger to gnash
His large teeth, ' I will flay
    Those young brutes when I thrash ! '
For the treacle had ruined his whiskers,
    And a small but much cherished moustache.

They had reason ere long
    Their rash act to deplore ;
His resentment was strong
    And he thirsted for gore.
So they each got a thundering licking,
    Which left them elated tho' sore.

For in spite of the pain,
    They had made it quite clear
That they never again
    Would let him domineer ;
And Jenkinson gained an ovation,
    When he called on the League for a cheer

Moral

Darkest clouds, we are told,
    Prove full oft silver-lined ;
So take heart and be bold,
    Even though you should find,
When you manfully cut them asunder,
    The stout ash-plant is lurking behind.

45

Likewise be not too swift
   The small boy to oppress ;
Lest his heart be uplift
   With a hope of success,
And he enter a vigorous protest,
   Which may land you at last in a mess.

DEAR Freddie,
      I am glad
  To hear you're feeling fitter—
Less like the pickled shad
  Who found this life so bitter.
And now I hope you'll grow
  In length and breadth and knowledge,
Until you climb to be in time
  A credit to the college.

At first a public school
  Is not a bed of roses;
A new boy feels a fool,
  And that the worst of woes is.
But if he is a pup,
  That's game, and not a clown, he
Soon learns to keep his pecker *up*
  And finds his bed more *downy*.

And now here's some advice
  Which will I hope be taken—
Avoid the penny ice,
  And too much eggs and bacon.
Work hard, but don't aspire
  (The copy-book gives warning)
To try to set the Thames on fire
  Too early in the morning.

A LETTER
OF ADVICE
TO F. S.
IN HIS FIRST
TERM AT A
PUBLIC
SCHOOL

47

Lock up your tin. Be slow
    To spend your last half dollar.
In form don't be too low
    Nor wear too high a collar.
Let all your actions strive
    To reach a lofty level ;
Work hard at Greek, and always speak
    The truth and shame the devil.

Don't get into a set
    Who make it their ambition
To smoke and drink and bet,
    Despite all prohibition.
For even cigarettes
    Have after all their drawbacks ;
And frequent pipes and secret swipes
    Are apt to lead to raw-backs.

Wear flannel next your skin,
    And cheat the mustard plaster,
Don't let your boots be thin,
    But such as the head-master
Has specially designed,
    For weather damp or freezing,
To save from woe the youthful toe,
    And put a stop to sneezing.

48

Shun as a general rule
   Unnecessary fighting,
And keep your temper cool,
   Black eyes look uninviting.
But if a beast's complaint
   Is insufficient licking—
A worthless brute who needs the boot
   And cries aloud for kicking ;

Then let your boots be thick
   (Be sure his hide is thicker)
Administer your kick
   As quick as thought, or quicker.
Reduce him to a pulp
   Like that which ring-tailed coons eat ;
And let your toe unerring go
   Straight for his pantaloon-seat.

Of course you're growing wise,
   Less cheeky and sedater.
I hope you'll get a prize
   To please the Gov. and Mater,
And now good-bye.   Keep straight,
   And never leave off wishing
To keep your name exempt from blame,
   Your latter end from swishing.

49

ONE cast in nature's noblest mould,
*   Pure type of innocence and joy,*
More precious than his weight in gold—
*   A simple, guileless English boy.*

She wandered about on the cricket field,
     Searching in vain for her darling son.
     There were plenty of boys, but alas not one
Who the longed-for features and form revealed.

She—aside.

I've looked in vain, till I'm ready to faint;
     What means to find him can I employ?
     I'll ask that beautiful blue-eyed boy,
With a face like an early-English saint.

He—aside.

Who can that funny old party be,
     Who seems, like an elderly little Bo-peep,
     To be looking about for a missing sheep?
And why in the world is she spotting me?

She—aloud.

You have got a most beautiful playground here,
     With its velvety turf and its shady trees;
     A boy would surely be hard to please
Who did not hold such a sweet place dear.

50

He—doubtfully.

Ye-es, not so bad as cricket grounds go,
　　But those beastly trees quite ruin the light;
　　And the turf, though, of course, it looks all right,
Is as dead as—I mean to say, precious slow.

She

I wonder whether you'd kindly try
　　To help me in finding my little Jo;
　　At least—but, of course, you could not know—
I believe in the lists he is called ' Jones mi.'

He

Oh, yes! I know.　With a freckled face,
　　And a nose the shape of a window peg.
　　He is commonly known as the 'addled-egg,'
And is probably down at the bathing-place.

She

I'm afraid I can't go and look for him there;
　　But possibly you'd be so very kind
　　As to go and see whether you can find
My boy, and tell him his mother's here.

He

Find him? of course.　I'll go like a shot,
　　And send him up to you right away,
　　It won't take a couple of shakes, and—eh?
Should I mind if you were to—? Ra-ather not !

51

She—aside.

What a beautiful boy! but what dreadful slang!
I trust that Jo has not learnt it too.
If he has, I shall scarcely know what to do.
It will cause me many a bitter pang.

He—as he goes.

Well, upon my word! what a rummy old frump!
Hulloa! why I'm blowed if I ever did!
She's been and tipped me a blooming quid!
Hanged if she isn't a regular trump!

WHEN I was a lad,' said grand-papa,
  'We used to have lots of fun;
It makes me chuckle still, ha, ha!
  To think how we took the bun!
Our neighbours would I'm sure agree
  That we were gay young sparks;
No boys were ever so fond of a spree,
  Or so often up to larks.'

'My grand-paternal relative,'
  Replied the youth in accents grave,
'Can you not see what pain you give,
  When you thus childishly behave?
Your boyish pranks might be excused,
  But slang I cannot overlook.
What was that dreadful phrase you used?
  What was it that you took?'

'Tut, tut,' the old man said, 'Pooh! pooh!
  Why what on earth's the row?
What are the young 'uns coming to,
  What *is* the matter now?
Lor bless my soul! Why, in my young days,
  A cheeky little brat like you,
Would have pretty soon learnt that the ass who
      brays,
  May be taught to say "Boo-hoo."'

LEGEND OF
THE GIDDY
GRAND-
FATHER,
AND THE
WISE
YOUTH,
HIS GRAND-
SON

53

'I cannot think how you can stoop
    To use those vulgar expletives,
More senseless than the frantic "whoop,"
    The "brave" upon the war-path gives.
Your hints at flogging too, no doubt,
    Are not at heart unkindly meant ;
But, in these days, we do without
    Degrading corporal punishment.'

At this the old man danced about,
    Like a bird on a bending twig.
His thin voice grew to a quavering shout
    As he screamed 'You little prig,
You ought to be whipped and sent to bed
    For treating your elders so ;
And if I'd my way, without delay
    To your bed-room you should go !'

'"How ill gray hairs become a fool!"
    Our glorious bard has wisely said,
A man should keep his temper cool,
    Unless he wants to lose his head.
Such ebullitions cannot fail
    To fill onlookers with contempt,
While self-control might well avail
    To keep a man from blame exempt'

' You dare to talk to me like that!
    What next I should like to know ?
You smug little canting meal-mouthed brat,
    Where do you expect to go ?
The boys, thank heaven ! when I was young
    Had not taken you for a guide;
And hadn't yet learnt to wrap their tongue
    Round words five syllables wide ! '

' My worthy old progenitor,
    You would do well to bear in mind
Your talk is very apt to bore
    Persons of intellect refined ;
And so henceforth I recommend
    That you your babble should subdue ;
And learn your manners to amend,
    By speaking when you're spoken to.'

THERE'S a branch of Her Majesty's subjects,
    A noisy and numerous band,
Who in tens and in hundreds of thousands   .
    Are scattered all over the land.
They are all of them keener than mustard,
    For their ardour no lethargy cools ;
And the people I mean to refer to
    Are the boys in our glorious schools.
                        Sing out !
    Our splendid unparalleled schools.

Oh, some compile notches at cricket,
    With their cuts and phenomenal drives,
And some get their colours for racquets,
    Or the more insignificant fives.
And some of them shine on the river,
    And some of them shout on the bank ;
For some are approved by the 'tubber,'
    But some are rejected as rank.
                        Outside !
    Quite wholly and hopelessly rank.

Some toil at quadratic equations,
    In search of the value of 'x' ;
And some do the double grand circle,
    At the imminent risk of their necks.

56

But somewhere and somehow and always,
    They have managed to make themselves heard;
From the sixth, with its four-in-hand prefects,
    To the game little songs in the IIIrd.
                        Hi there !
    You cheeky young fags in the IIIrd.

They have neatly bamboozled the masters,
    And have chaffed the unlucky Mossoo.
They have fastened his chair to his coat-tails,
    With a mixture of treacle and glue.
And when fell retribution has followed,
    In the shape of the sinuous cane,
They have cheerfully taken the licking,
    And done it all over again,
                        Oh dear !
    They have cobbler's-waxed it again.

They have mastered the metres of Horace,
    They have learned how to parry ' cut three,'
And to shin double-quick to the mast-head,
    Like a monkey that swarms up a tree.
They have learned to face peril unflinching,
    (For it's only a coward who runs !)

From the birch of an angry head-master,
  To the breath of the battery guns.
                        Quick march !
  To the pitiless roar of the guns.

They have taken their bulls-eyes at Bisley,
  They have run till they dropped in a ' grind.'
They have spurted in first for the ' Ladies,'
  Leaving Oxford and Cambridge behind.
No task is too great or ambitious,
  No mountain too steep or too high,
For the boys that don't know when they're beaten,
  And the pluck that will never say die,
                        Ride on,
  That is ready if need be to die.

They have furnished the army and navy
  With stalwart and resolute men.
And for one that's at present enlisted,
  They could send if we wanted them ten.
And it's known to the various nations
  Who with England may chance to have fought,
That the boys of J. B's little island
  Will give them as good as they brought
                        Ay, ay,
  Two or three times as good as they brought.

Then a health to the go-a-head schoolboys,
    Whose aims and ambitions are high !
Ne'er content till the pennon of England
    Above all other ensigns shall fly.
For be sure that whoever hereafter
    To the goal of his hopes shall attain,
Will look back with unqualified pleasure
    To the days of his boyhood again.
                        Come back !
The cane and the class-room again
                        Good biz.
The tips and the toffee again
                        Watch out.
The slide and toboggan again
                        Once more
The joys of our childhood again !

*F*OR *the use of the budding school-master. It is suggested that this be added, in the form of an appendix, to your already admirably phrased prospectus.*

A your Academy, name ever dear
For its classical sound to the middle-class ear.
B is the Boy, fond of Beef and of Buns,
Mem, describe in print always as 'gentlemen's
    sons.'
C stands for cheek; you'll need more than a trifle;
Not Conscience—for that you must carefully stifle.
D is the Drill, both for tall and for short meant,
Wherein all may acquire a fine martial Deportment.
E is your Eloquent Earnest Endeavour
To Encourage alike both the dull and the clever.
'*F* is Fonder of games than of work.' Thus you
    veil your
Real thoughts when you write of the Fool and the
    Failure.
G is the Good little Golden-haired boy
Who Grinds at his work with a Gander-like joy.
H is the House you describe as replete
With Home comforts—a Happy and Healthy
    Retreat.

I is the Idler's spasmodic Intention,
A fresh paving-stone—where? Well, it's best not
      to mention.
J the Judicious advice that you offer,
Described as a ' Jaw' by the infantine scoffer.
K is the place where your dear little chicks
Have been carefully grounded in—building with
      bricks.
L is your Look of disgust and dismay
At the Low-class establishment over the way.
M is the manners that Makyth the Man,
Not the Mercenary Motives, with which you began.
N is the New boy both nervous and shy,
Whose Nature will make itself known bye-and-
      bye.
O is the Oil and the Oxford Degree
Which will both come in handy at afternoon tea.
P is the Parent by Providence sent
The schoolmaster's numerous woes to augment.
Q are Quotations from Quintus H. Flaccus ;
Or allusions adriot to 'The Mother of Gracchus' ;
R—Richard's Report—your diplomacy tries!
Fill it up with—er—what's the polite word for
      ' lies?'
S is your System that's *so* Sympathetic,
Tho' to some tastes Soft Soap is a sloppy emetic.

T is your Temper that's somewhat uncertain,
Hence the whisper, 'Old Thunderstorm can't keep
      his shirt in ! '
U is the Usher, whose services cheaply
Are purchased ; so snub him, he won't feel it deeply.
V is your vanity, skilfully flattered,
Tho' at times rather rudely and painfully shattered.
W is your Wit, which you doubtless admire.
It is also the Wince that it's apt to inspire.
X is the symbol of value unknown
Whereby fitly your 'Great Expectations' are shown.
Y is the Yawn, which, imperfectly hidden,
Is the crushing reply of the boy you have chidden.
Z stands for Zimri.   No caution is needed
To warn you lest any boy treat you as he did.

THE END

JOHN LANE

THE
BODLEY
HEAD
VIGO St
W.
Telegrams
"BODLEIAN
LONDON"

E. NEW.

CATALOGUE of PUBLICATIONS
in BELLES LETTRES *all at net prices*

1895.

List of Books

IN

BELLES LETTRES

(*Including some Transfers*)

Published by John Lane

𝕿𝖍𝖊 𝕭𝖔𝖉𝖑𝖊𝖞 𝕳𝖊𝖆𝖉

VIGO STREET, LONDON, W.

N.B.—The Authors and Publisher reserve the right of reprinting any book in this list if a new edition is called for, except in cases where a stipulation has been made to the contrary, and of printing a separate edition of any of the books for America irrespective of the numbers to which the English editions are limited. The numbers mentioned do not include copies sent to the public libraries, nor those sent for review.

Most of the books are published simultaneously in England and America, and in many instances the names of the American Publishers are appended.

———◆———

ADAMS (FRANCIS).
 ESSAYS IN MODERNITY. Crown 8vo. 5s. net. [*Shortly*.
  Chicago: Stone & Kimball.
 A CHILD OF THE AGE. (*See* KEYNOTES SERIES.)
ALLEN (GRANT).
 THE LOWER SLOPES: A Volume of Verse. With Title-
  page and Cover Design by J. ILLINGWORTH KAY.
  600 copies. Crown 8vo. 5s. net.
  Chicago: Stone & Kimball.
 THE WOMAN WHO DID. (*See* KEYNOTES SERIES.)
 THE BRITISH BARBARIANS. (*See* KEYNOTES SERIES.)

BAILEY (JOHN C).
AN ANTHOLOGY OF ENGLISH ELEGIES. [*In preparation.*

BEARDSLEY (AUBREY).
THE STORY OF VENUS AND TANNHÄUSER, in which is set
forth an exact account of the Manner of State held by
Madam Venus, Goddess and Meretrix, under the
famous Hörselberg, and containing the adventures of
Tannhäuser in that place, his repentance, his jour-
neying to Rome, and return to the loving mountain.
By AUBREY BEARDSLEY. With 20 full-page Illustrations, numerous ornaments, and a cover from the
same hand. Sq. 16mo. 10s. 6d. net. [*In preparation.*

BEDDOES (T. L.).
See GOSSE (EDMUND).

BEECHING (REV. H. C.).
IN A GARDEN : Poems. With Title-page designed by
ROGER FRY. Crown 8vo. 5s. net.
New York : Macmillan & Co.

BENSON (ARTHUR CHRISTOPHER).
LYRICS. Fcap. 8vo, buckram. 5s. net.
New York : Macmillan & Co.

BRIDGES (ROBERT).
SUPPRESSED CHAPTERS AND OTHER BOOKISHNESS.
Crown 8vo. 3s. 6d. net.
New York : Charles Scribner's Sons.

BROTHERTON (MARY).
ROSEMARY FOR REMEMBRANCE. With Title-page and Cover
Design by WALTER WEST. Fcap. 8vo. 3s. 6d. net.

BUCHAN (JOHN).
MUSA PISCATRIX. 　　　　　　　　[*In preparation.*

CAMPBELL (GERALD).
   THE JONESES AND THE ASTERISKS.   (*See* MAYFAIR SET.)

CASE (ROBERT).
   AN ANTHOLOGY OF ENGLISH EPITHALAMIES.
   [In preparation.

CASTLE (MRS EGERTON).
   MY LITTLE LADY ANNE.   (*See* PIERROT'S LIBRARY.)

CASTLE (EGERTON).
   See STEVENSON (ROBERT LOUIS).

CRAIG (R. MANIFOLD).
   THE SACRIFICE OF FOOLS: A Novel.   Crown 8vo.
      4s. 6d. net.   *[In preparation.*

CRANE (WALTER).
   TOY BOOKS.   Re-issue.   Each with new Cover Design and
      end papers.   9d. net.
      The group of three bound in one volume, with a decora-
      tive cloth cover, end papers, and a newly written and
      designed preface.   3s. 6d. net.
      I. THIS LITTLE PIG.
      II. THE FAIRY SHIP.
      III. KING LUCKIEBOY'S PARTY.
         Chicago: Stone & Kimball.

CROSSE (VICTORIA).
   THE WOMAN WHO DIDN'T.   (*See* KEYNOTES SERIES.)

DALMON (C. W.).
   SONG FAVOURS.   With a Title-page designed by J. P.
      DONNE.   Sq. 16mo.   3s. 6d. net.
      Chicago: Way & Williams.

D'ARCY (ELLA).
   MONOCHROMES.   (*See* KEYNOTES SERIES.)

DAVIDSON (JOHN).

PLAYS: An Unhistorical Pastoral; A Romantic Farce; Bruce, a Chronicle Play; Smith, a Tragic Farce; Scaramouch in Naxos, a Pantomime, with a Frontispiece and Cover Design by AUBREY BEARDSLEY. Printed at the Ballantyne Press. 500 copies. Small 4to. 7s. 6d. net.
Chicago: Stone & Kimball.

FLEET STREET ECLOGUES. Fcap. 8vo, buckram. 5s. net. [*Out of Print at present.*

A RANDOM ITINERARY AND A BALLAD. With a Frontispiece and Title-page by LAURENCE HOUSMAN. 600 copies. Fcap. 8vo, Irish Linen. 5s. net.
Boston: Copeland & Day.

BALLADS AND SONGS. With a Title-page and Cover Design by WALTER WEST. Third Edition. Fcap. 8vo, buckram. 5s. net.
Boston: Copeland & Day.

DAWE (W. CARLTON).

YELLOW AND WHITE. (*See* KEYNOTES SERIES.)

DE TABLEY (LORD).

POEMS, DRAMATIC AND LYRICAL. By JOHN LEICESTER WARREN (Lord De Tabley). Illustrations and Cover Design by C. S. RICKETTS. Second Edition. Crown 8vo. 7s. 6d. net.
New York: Macmillan & Co.

POEMS, DRAMATIC AND LYRICAL. Second Series, uniform in binding with the former volume. Crown 8vo. 5s. net.
New York: Macmillan & Co.

DIX (GERTRUDE).

THE GIRL FROM THE FARM. (*See* KEYNOTES SERIES.)

DOSTOIEVSKY (F.).

See KEYNOTES SERIES, Vol. III.

ECHEGARAY (JOSÉ).
    See LYNCH (HANNAH).

EGERTON (GEORGE).
    KEYNOTES. (*See* KEYNOTES SERIES.)
    DISCORDS. (*See* KEYNOTES SERIES.)
    YOUNG OFEG'S DITTIES. A translation from the Swedish
       of OLA HANSSON. With Title-page and Cover Design
       by AUBREY BEARDSLEY. Crown 8vo. 3s. 6d. net.
          Boston : Roberts Bros.

FARR (FLORENCE).
    THE DANCING FAUN. (*See* KEYNOTES SERIES.)

FLEMING (GEORGE).
    FOR PLAIN WOMEN ONLY. (*See* MAYFAIR SET.)

FLETCHER (J. S.).
    THE WONDERFUL WAPENTAKE. By 'A SON OF THE
       SOIL.' With 18 full-page Illustrations by J. A.
       SYMINGTON. Crown 8vo. 5s. 6d. net.
          Chicago: A. C. McClurg & Co.

FREDERIC (HAROLD).
    MRS ALBERT GRUNDY. (*See* MAYFAIR SET.)

GALE (NORMAN).
    ORCHARD SONGS. With Title-page and Cover Design
       by J. ILLINGWORTH KAY. Fcap 8vo, Irish Linen.
       5s. net.
      Also a Special Edition limited in number on hand-made paper
      bound in English vellum. £1, 1s. net.
       New York : G. P. Putnam's Sons.

GARNETT (RICHARD).
    POEMS. With Title-page by J. ILLINGWORTH KAY.
       350 copies. Crown 8vo. 5s. net.
          Boston : Copeland & Day.
    DANTE, PETRARCH, CAMOENS, cxxiv Sonnets rendered
       in English. Crown 8vo. 5s. net. [*In preparation.*

GEARY (NEVILL).

> A LAWYER'S WIFE: A Novel. Crown 8vo. 4s. 6d.
> net. [*In preparation.*

GOSSE (EDMUND).

> THE LETTERS OF THOMAS LOVELL BEDDOES. Now
> first edited. Pott 8vo. 5s. net.
> Also 25 copies large paper. 12s. 6d. net.
> New York: Macmillan & Co.

GRAHAME (KENNETH).

> PAGAN PAPERS: A Volume of Essays. With Title-
> page by AUBREY BEARDSLEY. Fcap. 8vo. 5s. net.
> Chicago: Stone & Kimball.
> THE GOLDEN AGE. Crown 8vo. 3s. 6d. net.
> Chicago: Stone & Kimball.

GREENE (G. A.).

> ITALIAN LYRISTS OF TO-DAY. Translations in the
> original metres from about thirty-five living Italian
> poets, with bibliographical and biographical notes.
> Crown 8vo. 5s. net.
> New York: Macmillan & Co.

GREENWOOD (FREDERICK).

> IMAGINATION IN DREAMS. Crown 8vo. 5s. net.
> New York: Macmillan & Co.

HAKE (T. GORDON).

> A SELECTION FROM HIS POEMS. Edited by Mrs
> MEYNELL. With a Portrait after D. G. ROSSETTI,
> and a Cover Design by GLEESON WHITE. Crown
> 8vo. 5s. net.
> Chicago: Stone and Kimball.

HANSSON (LAURA MARHOLM).

> MODERN WOMEN: Six Psychological Sketches. [Sophia
> Kovalevsky, George Egerton, Eleanora Duse, Amalie
> Skram, Marie Bashkirtseff, A. Edgren Leffler.] Trans-
> lated from the German by HERMIONE RAMSDEN.
> Crown 8vo. 3s. 6d. net. [*In preparation.*

HANSSON (OLA).　*See* EGERTON.

HARLAND (HENRY).
>   GREY ROSES. (*See* KEYNOTES SERIES.)

HAYES (ALFRED).
>   THE VALE OF ARDEN AND OTHER POEMS. With a
>   Title-page and a Cover designed by E. H. NEW.
>   Fcap. 8vo. 3s. 6d. net.
>   Also 25 copies large paper. 15s. net.

HEINEMANN (WILLIAM).
>   THE FIRST STEP. A Dramatic Moment. Small 4to.
>   3s. 6d. net.

HOPPER (NORA).
>   BALLADS IN PROSE. With a Title-page and Cover by
>   WALTER WEST. Sq. 16mo. 5s. net.
>   Boston : Roberts Bros.
>   A VOLUME OF POEMS. With Title-page designed by
>   PATTEN WILSON. Sq. 16mo. 5s. net.
>   *[In preparation.*

HOUSMAN (CLEMENCE).
>   THE WERE WOLF. With six Full-page Illustrations,
>   Title-page and Cover Design, by LAURENCE HOUS-
>   MAN. Sq. 16mo. 4s. net. *[In preparation.*

HOUSMAN (LAURENCE).
>   GREEN ARRAS : Poems. With Illustrations by the
>   Author. Crown 8vo. 5s. net. *[In preparation.*

IRVING (LAURENCE).
>   GODEFROI AND YOLANDE : A Play. With three Illus-
>   trations by AUBREY BEARDSLEY. Sm. 4to. 5s. net.
>   *[In preparation.*

JAMES (W. P.).
>   ROMANTIC PROFESSIONS : A Volume of Essays. With
>   Title - page designed by J. ILLINGWORTH KAY.
>   Crown 8vo. 5s. net.
>   New York : Macmillan & Co.

JOHNSON (LIONEL).

THE ART OF THOMAS HARDY : Six Essays. With Etched
Portrait by WM. STRANG, and Bibliography by JOHN
LANE. Second Edition. Crown 8vo. 5s. 6d. net.
Also 150 copies, large paper, with proofs of the portrait. £1, 1s.
net.
New York : Dodd, Mead & Co.

JOHNSON (PAULINE).

WHITE WAMPUM : Poems. With a Title-page and Cover
Design by E. H. NEW. Crown 8vo. 5s. net.
Boston : Lamson, Wolffe & Co.

JOHNSTONE (C. E.).

BALLADS OF BOY AND BEAK. With a Title-page designed
by F. II. TOWNSEND. Sq. 32mo. 2s. 6d. net.
[*In preparation.*

KEYNOTES SERIES.

Each volume with specially designed Title-page by AUBREY
BEARDSLEY. Crown 8vo, cloth. 3s. 6d. net.

Vol. I. KEYNOTES. By GEORGE EGERTON.
[*Seventh edition now ready.*
Vol. II. THE DANCING FAUN. By FLORENCE FARR.
Vol. III. POOR FOLK. Translated from the Russian of
F. Dostoievsky by LENA MILMAN. With a Preface
by GEORGE MOORE.
Vol. IV. A CHILD OF THE AGE. By FRANCIS ADAMS.
Vol. V. THE GREAT GOD PAN AND THE INMOST
LIGHT. By ARTHUR MACHEN.
[*Second edition now ready.*
Vol. VI. DISCORDS. By GEORGE EGERTON.
[*Fourth edition now ready.*
Vol. VII. PRINCE ZALESKI. By M. P. SHIEL.
Vol. VIII. THE WOMAN WHO DID. By GRANT ALLEN.
[*Eighteenth edition now ready.*

KEYNOTES SERIES—*continued.*
  Vol.   IX. WOMEN'S TRAGEDIES. By H. D. LOWRY.
  Vol.   X. GREY ROSES. By HENRY HARLAND.
  Vol.   XI. AT THE FIRST CORNER AND OTHER STORIES.
     By H. B. MARRIOTT WATSON.
  Vol.   XII. MONOCHROMES. By ELLA D'ARCY.
  Vol. XIII. AT THE RELTON ARMS. By EVELYN SHARP.
  Vol. XIV. THE GIRL FROM THE FARM. By GERTRUDE
     DIX.
  Vol. XV. THE MIRROR OF MUSIC. By STANLEY V.
     MAKOWER.
  Vol. XVI. YELLOW AND WHITE. By W. CARLTON
     DAWE.
  Vol. XVII. THE MOUNTAIN LOVERS. By FIONA
     MACLEOD.
  Vol. XVIII. THE WOMAN WHO DIDN'T. By VICTORIA
     CROSSE.   *[Second edition now ready.*
      The following are in rapid preparation.
  Vol. XIX. THE THREE IMPOSTORS. By ARTHUR
     MACHEN.
  Vol. XX. NOBODY'S FAULT. By NETTA SYRETT.
  Vol. XXI. THE BRITISH BARBARIANS. By GRANT ALLEN.
  Vol. XXII. IN HOMESPUN. By E. NESBIT.
  Vol. XXIII. PLATONIC AFFECTIONS. By JOHN SMITH.
  Vol. XXIV. NETS FOR THE WIND. By UNA TAYLOR.
  Vol. XXV. ORANGE AND GREEN. By CALDWELL LIP-
     SETT.
        Boston : Roberts Bros.

KING (MAUDE EGERTON).
  ROUND ABOUT A BRIGHTON COACH OFFICE. With 30
     Illustrations by LUCY KEMP WELCH. Cr. 8vo.
     5s. net.   *[In preparation.*
LANDER (HARRY).
  WEIGHED IN THE BALANCE : A Novel. Crown 8vo.
     4s. 6d. net   *[In preparation.*

LANG (ANDREW). *See* STODDART.

LEATHER (R. K.).

    VERSES. 250 copies. Fcap. 8vo. 3s. net.
      Transferred by the Author to the present Publisher.

LE GALLIENNE (RICHARD).

    PROSE FANCIES. With Portrait of the Author by
      WILSON STEER. Fourth Edition. Crown 8vo.
      Purple cloth. 5s. net.
    Also a limited large paper edition. 12s. 6d. net.
      New York: G. P. Putnam's Sons.

    THE BOOK BILLS OF NARCISSUS, An Account rendered
      by RICHARD LE GALLIENNE. Third Edition. With
      a Frontispiece. Crown 8vo. Purple cloth. 3s. 6d. net.
    Also 50 copies on large paper. 8vo. 10s. 6d. net.
      New York: G. P. Putnam's Sons.

    ROBERT LOUIS STEVENSON, AN ELEGY, AND OTHER
      POEMS, MAINLY PERSONAL. With Etched Title-page
      by D. Y. CAMERON. Cr. 8vo. Purple cloth. 4s. 6d. net.
    Also 75 copies on large paper. 8vo. 12s. 6d. net.
      Boston: Copeland & Day.

    ENGLISH POEMS. Fourth Edition, revised. Crown 8vo.
      Purple cloth. 4s. 6d. net.
      Boston: Copeland & Day.

LE GALLIENNE (RICHARD).

    RETROSPECTIVE REVIEWS, A LITERARY LOG, 1891-1895.
      2 vols. crown 8vo. Purple cloth. 9s. net.
                          [In preparation.
      New York: Dodd, Mead & Co.

    GEORGE MEREDITH: Some Characteristics. With a Biblio-
      graphy (much enlarged) by JOHN LANE, Portrait, etc.
      Fourth Edition. Cr. 8vo. Purple cloth. 5s. 6d. net.

    THE RELIGION OF A LITERARY MAN. 5th thousand.
      Crown 8vo. Purple cloth. 3s. 6d. net.
    Also a special rubricated edition on hand-made paper. 8vo.
    10s. 6d. net.
      New York: G. P. Putnam's Sons.

LIPSETT (CALDWELL).
  ORANGE AND GREEN.   (*See* KEYNOTES SERIES.)
LOWRY (H. D.).
  WOMEN'S TRAGEDIES.   (*See* KEYNOTES SERIES.)
LUCAS (WINIFRED).
  A VOLUME OF POEMS.   Fcap. 8vo.   4s. 6d. net.
                                        [*In preparation.*
LYNCH (HANNAH).
  THE GREAT GALEOTO AND FOLLY OR SAINTLINESS.   TWO
    Plays, from the Spanish of JOSÉ ECHEGARAY, with an
    Introduction.   Small 4to.   5s. 6d. net.
      Boston : Lamson, Wolffe & Co.

MACHEN (ARTHUR).
  THE GREAT GOD PAN.   (*See* KEYNOTES SERIES.)
  THE THREE IMPOSTORS.   (*See* KEYNOTES SERIES.)
MACLEOD (FIONA).
  THE MOUNTAIN LOVERS.   (*See* KEYNOTES SERIES.)
MAKOWER (STANLEY V.).
  THE MIRROR OF MUSIC.   (*See* KEYNOTES SERIES.)
MARZIALS (THEO.).
  THE GALLERY OF PIGEONS AND OTHER POEMS.   Post
    8vo.   4s. 6d. net.   [*Very few remain.*
      Transferred by the Author to the present Publisher.

MATHEW (FRANK).
  THE WOOD OF THE BRAMBLES : A Novel.   Crown 8vo.
    4s. 6d. net.   [*In preparation.*
THE MAYFAIR SET.
  Each volume fcap. 8vo.   3s. 6d. net.
  Vol. I. THE AUTOBIOGRAPHY OF A BOY : Passages
    selected by his Friend, G. S. STREET.   With a Title-
    page designed by C. W. FURSE.
                          [*Fourth Edition now ready.*

THE MAYFAIR SET—*continued*

Vol. II. THE JONESES AND THE ASTERISKS: a Story in Monologue. By GERALD CAMPBELL. With Title-page and six Illustrations by F. H. TOWNSEND.

Vol. III. SELECT CONVERSATIONS WITH AN UNCLE NOW EXTINCT. By H. G. WELLS. With Title-page by F. H. TOWNSEND.

The following are in preparation.

Vol. IV. THE FEASTS OF AUTOLYCUS: The Diary of a Greedy Woman. Edited by ELIZABETH ROBINS PENNELL.

Vol. V. MRS ALBERT GRUNDY: Observations in Philistia. By HAROLD FREDERIC.

Vol. VI. FOR PLAIN WOMEN ONLY. By GEORGE FLEMING.

New York : The Merriam Company.

MEREDITH (GEORGE).

THE FIRST PUBLISHED PORTRAIT OF THIS AUTHOR, engraved on the wood by W. BISCOMBE GARDNER, after the painting by G. F. WATTS. Proof copies on Japanese vellum, signed by painter and engraver. £1, 1s. net.

MEYNELL (MRS.), (ALICE C. THOMPSON).

POEMS. Fcap. 8vo. 3s. 6d. net. [*Out of Print at present.*
A few of the 50 large paper copies (First Edition) remain, 12s. 6d. net.

THE RHYTHM OF LIFE AND OTHER ESSAYS. Second Edition. Fcap. 8vo. 3s. 6d. net.
A few of the 50 large paper copies (First Edition) remain, 12s. 6d. net.

See also HAKE.

MILLER (JOAQUIN).

THE BUILDING OF THE CITY BEAUTIFUL. Fcap. 8vo. With a Decorated Cover. 5s. net.

Chicago : Stone & Kimball.

MILMAN (LENA).

DOSTOIEVSKY'S POOR FOLK. (*See* KEYNOTES SERIES.)

MONKHOUSE (ALLAN).

BOOKS AND PLAYS : A Volume of Essays on Meredith, Borrow, Ibsen, and others. 400 copies. Crown 8vo. 5s. net.
Philadelphia : J. B. Lippincott Co.

MOORE (GEORGE).

See KEYNOTES SERIES, Vol. III.

NESBIT (E.).

A POMANDER OF VERSE. With a Title-page and Cover designed by LAURENCE HOUSMAN. Crown 8vo. 5s. net.
Chicago : A. C. McClurg & Co.
IN HOMESPUN. (*See* KEYNOTES SERIES.)

NETTLESHIP (J. T.).

ROBERT BROWNING : Essays and Thoughts. Third Edition. With a Portrait. Crown 8vo. 5s. 6d. net.
New York : Chas. Scribner's Sons.

NOBLE (JAS. ASHCROFT).

THE SONNET IN ENGLAND AND OTHER ESSAYS. Title-page and Cover Design by AUSTIN YOUNG. 600 copies. Crown 8vo. 5s. net.
Also 50 copies large paper. 12s. 6d. net.

O'SHAUGHNESSY (ARTHUR).

HIS LIFE AND HIS WORK. With Selections from his Poems. By LOUISE CHANDLER MOULTON. Portrait and Cover Design. Fcap. 8vo. 5s. net.
Chicago : Stone & Kimball.

OXFORD CHARACTERS.

A series of lithographed portraits by WILL ROTHENSTEIN, with text by F. YORK POWELL and others. To be issued monthly in term. Each number will contain two portraits. Parts I. to VI. ready. 200 sets only, folio, wrapper, 5s. net per part; 25 special large paper sets containing proof impressions of the portraits signed by the artist, 10s. 6d. net per part.

PENNELL (ELIZABETH ROBINS).

THE FEASTS OF AUTOLYCUS. (*See* MAYFAIR SET.)

PETERS (WM. THEODORE).

POSIES OUT OF RINGS. Sq. 16mo. 3s. 6d. net.
[*In preparation.*

PIERROT'S LIBRARY.

Each volume with Title-page, Cover Design, and End-papers designed by AUBREY BEARDSLEY. Sq. 16mo. 2s. 6d. net.
The following are in preparation.
Vol. I. PIERROT. By H. DE VERE STACPOOLE.
Vol. II. MY LITTLE LADY ANNE. By Mrs EGERTON CASTLE.
Vol. III. DEATH, THE KNIGHT AND THE LADY. By H. DE VERE STACPOOLE.
Vol. IV. SIMPLICITY. By A. T. G. PRICE.
   Philadelphia : Henry Altemus.

PISSARRO (LUCIEN).

THE QUEEN OF THE FISHES. A Story of the Valois, adapted by MARGARET RUST, being a printed manuscript, decorated with pictures and other ornaments, cut on the wood by LUCIEN PISSARO, and printed by him in divers colours and in gold at his press in Epping. Edition limited to 70 copies, each numbered and signed. Crown 8vo, on Japanese handmade paper, bound in vellum, £1 net.

PLARR (VICTOR).
>   In the Dorian Mood : Poems.   Crown 8vo.   5s. net.
>   [*In preparation.*

PRICE (A. T. G.).
>   Simplicity.   (*See* Pierrot's Library.)

RADFORD (DOLLIE).
>   Songs and other Verses.   With Title-page designed
>   by Patten Wilson.   Fcap. 8vo.   4s. 6d. net.
>   Philadelphia : J. B. Lippincott Co.

RAMSDEN (HERMIONE).
>   *See* Hansson.

RICKETTS (C. S.) and C. H. SHANNON.
>   Hero and Leander.   By Christopher Marlowe
>   and George Chapman.   With Borders, Initials, and
>   Illustrations designed and engraved on the wood by
>   C. S. Ricketts and C. H. Shannon.   Bound in
>   English vellum and gold.   200 copies only.   35s. net.
>   Boston : Copeland & Day.

RHYS (ERNEST).
>   A London Rose and other Rhymes.   With Title-page
>   designed by Selwyn Image.   350 copies.   Crown
>   8vo.   5s. net.
>   New York : Dodd, Mead & Co.

ROBERTSON (JOHN M.).
>   Essays towards a Critical Method.   (New Series.)
>   Crown 8vo.   5s. net.   [*In preparation.*

ROBINSON (C. NEWTON).
>   The Viol of Love.   With Ornaments and Cover Design
>   by Laurence Housman.   Crown 8vo.   5s. net.
>   Boston : Lamson, Wolffe & Co.

ST. CYRES (LORD).
>   The Little Flowers of St. Francis : A new ren-
>   dering into English of the Fioretti di San Francesco.
>   Crown 8vo.   5s. net.   [*In preparation.*

SHARP (EVELYN).
AT THE RELTON ARMS. (*See* KEYNOTES SERIES.)

SHIEL (M. P.).
PRINCE ZALESKI. (*See* KEYNOTES SERIES.)

SMITH (JOHN).
PLATONIC AFFECTIONS. (*See* KEYNOTES SERIES.)

STACPOOLE (H. DE VERE).
PIERROT. (*See* PIERROT'S LIBRARY.)
DEATH, THE KNIGHT AND THE LADY. (*See* PIERROT'S LIBRARY.)

STEVENSON (ROBERT LOUIS).
PRINCE OTTO. A rendering in French by EGERTON CASTLE. Crown 8vo. 5s. net. [*In preparation.*
Also 100 copies on large paper, uniform in size with the Edinburgh Edition of the Works.
A CHILD'S GARDEN OF VERSES. With nearly 100 Illustrations by CHARLES ROBINSON. Crown 8vo. 5s. net. [*In preparation.*

STODDART (THOS. TOD).
THE DEATH WAKE. With an Introduction by ANDREW LANG. Fcap. 8vo. 5s. net.
Chicago: Way & Williams.

STREET (G. S.).
THE AUTOBIOGRAPHY OF A BOY. (*See* MAYFAIR SET.)
MINIATURES AND MOODS. Fcap. 8vo. 3s. net.
Transferred by the Author to the present Publisher.
New York: The Merriam Co.

SWETTENHAM (F. A.).
MALAY SKETCHES. With Title-page and Cover Design by PATTEN WILSON. Crown 8vo. 5s. net.
New York: Macmillan & Co.

SYRETT (NETTA).

NOBODY'S FAULT. (*See* KEYNOTES SERIES.)

TABB (JOHN B.).

POEMS. Sq. 32mo. 4s. 6d. net.
Boston : Copeland & Day.

TAYLOR (UNA).

NETS FOR THE WIND. (*See* KEYNOTES SERIES.)

TENNYSON (FREDERICK).

POEMS OF THE DAY AND YEAR. With a Title-page by
PATTEN WILSON. Crown 8vo. 5s. net.
Chicago : Stone & Kimball.

THIMM (C. A.).

A COMPLETE BIBLIOGRAPHY OF THE ART OF FENCE,
DUELLING, ETC. With Illustrations. [*In preparation.*

THOMPSON (FRANCIS).

POEMS. With Frontispiece, Title-page, and Cover Design
by LAURENCE HOUSMAN. Fourth Edition. Pott
4to. 5s. net.
Boston : Copeland & Day.

SISTER SONGS : An Offering to Two Sisters. With Frontis-
piece, Title-page, and Cover Design by LAURENCE
HOUSMAN. Pott 4to. 5s. net.
Boston : Copeland & Day.

THOREAU (HENRY DAVID).

POEMS OF NATURE. Selected and edited by HENRY S.
SALT and FRANK B. SANBORN, with a Title-page
designed by PATTEN WILSON. Fcap. 8vo. 4s. 6d.
net. [*In preparation.*
Boston and New York : Houghton, Mifflin & Co.

TYNAN HINKSON (KATHARINE).

CUCKOO SONGS. With Title-page and Cover Design by
LAURENCE HOUSMAN. Fcap. 8vo. 5s. net.
Boston : Copeland & Day.

MIRACLE PLAYS: OUR LORD'S COMING AND CHILDHOOD.
With Six Illustrations and a Title-page by PATTEN
WILSON. Fcap. 8vo. net. [*In preparation.*
Chicago : Stone & Kimball.

WATSON (ROSAMUND MARRIOTT).

VESPERTILIA AND OTHER POEMS. With a Title-page
designed by R. ANNING BELL. Fcap. 8vo. 4s. 6d.
net.

A SUMMER NIGHT AND OTHER POEMS. New edition,
with a decorative Title-page. Fcap. 8vo. 3s. net.
Chicago : Way & Williams. [*In preparation.*

WATSON (H. B. MARRIOTT).

AT THE FIRST CORNER. (*See* KEYNOTES SERIES.)
THE KING'S HIGHWAY. Crown 8vo. 4s. 6d. net.
[*In preparation.*

WATSON (WILLIAM).

ODES AND OTHER POEMS. Fourth Edition. Fcap. 8vo,
buckram. 4s. 6d. net.
New York : Macmillan & Co.

THE ELOPING ANGELS : A Caprice. Second Edition.
Square 16mo, buckram. 3s. 6d. net.
New York : Macmillan & Co.

EXCURSIONS IN CRITICISM : being some Prose Recrea-
tions of a Rhymer. Second Edition. Cr. 8vo. 5s. net.
New York : Macmillan & Co.

THE PRINCE'S QUEST AND OTHER POEMS. With a
Bibliographical Note added. Second Edition. Fcap.
8vo. 4s. 6d. net.

WATT (FRANCIS).

THE LAW'S LUMBER ROOM. Fcap. 8vo. 3s. 6d. net.
Chicago : A. C. McClurg & Co.

WATTS (THEODORE).

POEMS. Crown 8vo. 5s. net. *[In preparation.*
There will also be an Edition de Luxe *of this volume printed at
the Kelmscott Press.*

WELLS (H. G.).

SELECT CONVERSATIONS WITH AN UNCLE. (*See* MAY-
FAIR SET.)

WHARTON (H. T.).

SAPPHO. Memoir, Text, Selected Renderings, and
Literal Translation by HENRY THORNTON WHARTON.
With three Illustrations in Photogravure, and a Cover
designed by AUBREY BEARDSLEY. Fcap. 8vo.
7s. 6d. net.
Chicago : A. C. McClurg & Co.

THE YELLOW BOOK

An Illustrated Quarterly

Pott 4to.   5s. net.

VOLUME I.   April 1894.   272 pages.   15 Illustrations.
[Out of print.
VOLUME II.   July 1894.   364 pages.   23 Illustrations.
VOLUME III.   October 1894.   280 pages.   15 Illustrations.
VOLUME IV.   January 1895.   285 pages.   16 Illustrations.
VOLUME V.   April 1895.   317 pages.   14 Illustrations.
VOLUME VI.   July 1895.   335 pages.   16 Illustrations.
Boston : Copeland & Day.